Turtle and Snake's Day at the Beach

A Viking Easy-to-Read

by Kate Spohn

VIKING

For Tiggy with love

VIKING
Published by the Penguin Group
Penguin Putnam Books for Young Readers,
345 Hudson Street, New York, New York 10014, U.S.A.
Penguin Books Ltd, 80 Strand, London WC2R 0RL, England
Penguin Books Australia Ltd, 250 Camberwell Road, Camberwell, Victoria 3124, Australia
Penguin Books Canada Ltd, 10 Alcorn Avenue, Toronto, Ontario, Canada M4V 3B2
Penguin Books (N.Z.) Ltd, 182-190 Wairau Road, Auckland 10, New Zealand

Penguin Books Ltd, Registered Offices: Harmondsworth, Middlesex, England

First published in 2003 by Viking,
a division of Penguin Putnam Books for Young Readers.

1 3 5 7 9 10 8 6 4 2

LIBRARY OF CONGRESS CATALOGING-IN-PUBLICATION DATA
Spohn, Kate.
Turtle and Snake's day at the beach / by Kate Spohn.
p. cm.
Summary: Turtle and Snake go to the beach, where they and some other
animals participate in a sandcastle-making contest.
ISBN 0-670-03628-5 (hardcover)
[1. Beaches—Fiction. 2. Sandcastles—Fiction. 3. Contests—Fiction.
4. Turtles—Fiction. 5. Snakes—Fiction. 6. Animals—Fiction.] I. Title.
PZ7.S7636 Tw 2003
[E]—dc21
2002153376

Printed in Hong Kong
Set in Bookman

Reading Level 1.9

Turtle and Snake are going
to the beach.

They pack towels,

an umbrella,

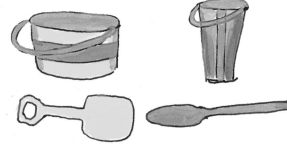

pails and
shovels,

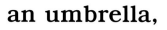

and surfboards.

Let's go!

"Look," says Turtle.

"Let's enter the contest,"
says Snake.

First, Turtle and Snake
find the perfect spot.

Next, they set up the umbrella
and unpack their beach things.

Then, it's time to start their
sand castle!
They dig, dig, dig.

And they pat, pat, pat.

"It's perfect!" says Turtle.

"I'm hot," says Snake.

"Let's surf!" says Turtle.

Turtle and Snake
ride the waves.

Oh no, Snake. Watch out!

Wipeout!

Turtle and Snake go back to
their umbrella.
Oh no! Where did the sand
castle go?

Time to build a new sand
castle.
They dig, dig, dig.
And they pat, pat, pat.

18

"It's perfect!" says Snake.

"Let's look for seashells,"
says Turtle.

Turtle and Snake collect lots
of shells.
But when they go back to
their umbrella . . .

Oh no! Look at that wave!

"Don't worry," says Snake.
"We'll feel better after some
ice cream."

Much better!

25

Oh no! Look at the time!
It's almost three o'clock.

"What will we do?" asks Turtle.
"We don't have a sand castle,"
says Snake.

"Don't worry," says Cat.
"We'll all help!"

So they dig, dig, dig.

And they pat, pat, pat.

Will Turtle and Snake win
a prize?

Everyone wins a prize!